WHO TOLD THE MOST INCREDIBI

HOW DOG'S NOSE BECAME DARK AND OTHER STORIES

Naana J.E.S. Opoku-Agyemang

VOLUME 1

Afram Publications (Ghana) Limited

Published by:
Afram Publications (Ghana) Limited
P.O. Box M18
Accra, Ghana

Tel: +233 302 412 561, +233 244 314 103
Kumasi: +233 322 047 524/5
E-mail: sales@aframpubghana.com
             publishing@aframpubghana.com
Website: www.aframpubghana.com

First Published, 2015
ISBN: 9964 70 533 6

Edited by: Adwoa A. Opoku-Agyemang
Illustrated by: Peter "Poka" Asamoa

Content

HOW DOG'S NOSE BECAME DARK

In a household in a faraway place, Dog, Hen and Goat lived with human beings. The people were generally tolerant and the animals lived in near-harmony with them. Dog was the happiest animal of all three because he was never killed for food. The worst fortune he suffered was to have his puppies given away as gifts to other households; but since this separation occurred within the same community, there was always a chance of meeting his children again. Hen and Goat were not so fortunate. However, they excused their predicament by reasoning that it was better than living in the forest with wild animals that would kill them for food even while a goat suckled her kids or a hen brooded her eggs.

One day the three animals went to work on their farms. Hen held her hoe with both hands and scraped away at the weeds which grew between the groundnut plants. With his left hand Dog held a stick with a curved end with which he parted the tall grass, while with his right hand he cut the weeds as close to the roots as he could manage it. While the two of them were weeding, Goat collected firewood and picked avocado pears. They worked until the position of the sun in the sky told them it was time to take a break.

They then brought out some cocoyam to roast on the open fire, and they started a discussion about their lives in the household. They were generally contented, but one thing disturbed them deeply:

"All the people of the house have proper names" Goat started, "apart from us. No one in this house is simply called Human Being. Indeed, people have numerous names and titles."

"To begin with, each person has a day name," continued Hen. "The first name is determined by the day of the week on which a person is born. So if a boy is born on a Wednesday he is called Kweku; a girl born on the same day will be known as Ekua. Then comes a second name which is given the day the child is brought outdoors for the first time. I have observed that this ceremony is usually performed on the eighth day after its birth. I can't overlook this event because people always kill one of our kinsmen for the celebration."

Dog continued with the subject: "I am generally allowed close to people so I know a little bit more about their practices. The second name is chosen from either side of the child's family. The child is supposed to live a life similar to that of his or her predecessor. You can understand how they eliminate the irresponsible ones from the family register. So this male child to whom Hen just referred may be called Kweku Brefo because the grandfather who was kind, generous and intelligent was called Brefo. The child may also have another name depending on the number of children his mother has   if he is the second boy in a row he may be called Manu in addition to his other names, for example, Kweku Manu Brefo. Or, children may be given the titles Maame, Eno, Awo, Papa, Egya or Nana, depending on whether they are named after their parent's parent or grandparent. This child may thus end up with a name like Papa Kweku Manu Brefo. So each person has at least two names; most have three."

"In addition to all the names that a man or a woman may have, they are sometimes called by the names of their children, so that Kweku Asamoa who is the father of Kwabena Dankwa is sometimes called Kwabena Papa, and so on," went on Dog to enlighten his friends.

"I understand that in other cultures a child takes on his father's name automatically," Goat said.

"What will be the sense in that?" asked Hen. "I mean, I agree with the practice that a person must lead a life worthy of emulation to have a child named for him.

If the child automatically takes the father's name it means he does not even have to try to be a responsible father. The last time Opanyin Kwasi Kra was performing libation, he refused to call on the name of Kwame Donkor. Donkor was mean, callous and selfish. Everyone knows how he never wasted an opportunity to remind the people living at the other side of the ridge that they did not be belong here, that they were people abandoned by their own ancestors. Donkor also pawned family lands in order to keep up litigation over the successor to the previous chief, Nana Kobena Bona. Do you mean that a man like Donkor would already have had children named for him? Who wants a duplication of such a life?"

"Not necessarily so," Goat interjected. "Obviously, if the child answers by the father's name I think a great sense of obligation would have been bestowed on the father to morally educate his child. People like Donkor are intractable and are better left alone even while libation is being performed. He would be too busy answering charges and being flogged before the ancestors; he would have neither the capacity nor the time to respond to the needs of the living anyway… But in our own cases we are called Goat, Hen, and Dog."

"Yes, it is a method of naming that suggests that we have no past. We should do something about it, and soon," Hen advised.

The animals debated a little longer about the significance of names and naming, and they came to the conclusion that since they did not have names in their respective families from which they could choose, they would give themselves new names. Human beings did not have to drum their own names and praises, because they already had a system in place for naming. Hen began:

"From now on, I want to be known as Amoaa Awisi, the woman with many children of her own but who raised those of others as well."

"From now on," Dog took up the cue, "I want to be known as Kwasi Wusu, the valiant one who brought the village back to life."

"As for me," proclaimed Goat, I want to be known as Kofi Apau, the one who overpowers bullets in times of war."

The animals were delighted by the names they had given themselves, and it showed! Suddenly they started to feel a measure of self-confidence they had not experienced before. The names seemed to have instantly elevated them from the rank of objects to identifiable beings. They were not very successful at hiding their newfound pride, since they danced and made a lot of noise on their way home. Dog led the team, yapping away as Hen cackled wildly; Goat bleated with his

mouth open so wide that you could count all his teeth and see your way right
down his throat into his stomach.

People came out of their houses to see what was going on. Some thought a dangerous snake was lurking by. Others felt Hen had started the usual noise after laying an egg and that she had overdone it this time, causing the other animals to react with fright. But having calmed down before the day ended, the animals resolved to keep the names a secret lest the people of the house got upset with them for giving themselves such airs. The reaction they had received earlier on was a clear indication that mankind would not take very kindly to their new names.

What became apparent to everyone was that from that afternoon when the three of them disturbed the community with their noisy entry, the animals spent more time with each other than usual. They were seen in deep discussion most of the time, but people decided just to leave them alone.

One day, while Hen pecked at a couple of groundnuts which had fallen from the cane basket, a woman shouted at her: "Just move off, you Hen. You really have become too much even for yourself. Since when do you feed on groundnuts? Though come to think of it, why should I be surprised. Since you started calling yourself Amoaa Awisi you have lost sight of reality. So you are the great breast that feeds its own and nurtures others as well! Ha! Didn't I see you the other day fighting with your own brood over a rotten piece of cassava? Is that how you look after your own as well as the offspring of others like Amoaa Awisi? You have no shame. Move yourself out of my sight before I determine what to give the medicine man to pacify my soul."

Hen was so shocked and frightened that there was nothing she could do. Who could have disclosed the information? That late afternoon when the three of them met under the awning, she decided to ask the others:

"My friends, it looks like the inhabitants of the house know my new name. And just as we predicted, we are not going to be the better for it. I can swear by that fateful day on which my husband the handsome cock was horrifically slaughtered that I had nothing to do with it. Why would I provide information which is only good for making my life miserable?'

Goat replied by saying: "Hen, do not upset yourself unduly. I was thinking of calling a meeting to discuss the same subject. Just about two days ago, I went by the neem tree to rub my skin against its bark, since I was suffering from an awful itch. Can you imagine what the hunter who was polishing his gun told me? I know you don't because you were not there, so listen. He said: 'You good for nothing

Goat. You call yourself Kofi Apau, the one who overcomes bullets, yet you scratch yourself like an animal. Who put that idea into your head? Can you fancy yourself as a member of an army when you cannot even put out a fire in the kitchen? And whose war would a goat be fighting? I know your kind: you wait till the men have left home so that you can intimidate the women. If you don't disappear by the time I bat my eyes I will give you a kick which will rearrange your brains so that you can start to behave like a proper goat again. Kofi Apau! Ah Goat, when Naked Man promises to give you a piece of cloth, just ask him to repeat his name.' Yes! These insults and many more. He was so angry that I thought he was going to shoot me! Now, only the three of us were at the farm when we gave ourselves those names. Who has betrayed our secret despite our agreement to the contrary?"

"Oh, this is strange indeed," started Dog in whose direction both Hen and Goat had turned their eyes. "I was lying beside the chair in the outer room when the oldest child of the fisherman, the insolent one, asked me to go and sleep in the ashes of the hearth! He went on that having called myself Kwasi Wusu I was likely to demand to be made chief for my assertion of bringing the village back to life. He said so many other nasty things about me including accusing me of mating with the woman who gave birth to me and asked how any thinking person would consider me for leader. So stop looking at me that way because I did not double-cross you."

"And I have nothing to do with the betrayal," said the Goat.

"Don't even look this way because it wasn't me," Hen vowed.

After much discussion and denial the animals agreed they have to out by all means who was the traitor among them. So they all went back to the farm and made a huge fire with dry twigs and parched corn husks which quickly burst into flames. The terms were that each animal would jump over the fire, and the traitor would end up with burns. Hen offered to go first. She started a song by giving a call to which the other two responded:

It's me Amoaa Awisi

It's me, oh, it's me

We went to the farm

It's me, oh, it's me

And gave ourselves names

It's me, oh, it's me

> If I am the one who
> Let out the secret
> It's me, oh, it's me
> May the fire burn me
> It's me, oh, it's me

After the last response Hen jumped and crossed the fire without any injury, thereby proving her innocence. Goat also sang and jumped over the fire without a single blister. Although by this time it was apparent that Dog was the one who had revealed the secret, it was only proper that he be given a chance like everyone else. Dog confidently took his turn, raised his snout up to the sky and started to sing:

> It's me Kwasi Wusu
> It's me, oh, it's me
> We, went to the farm
> It's me, oh, it's me
> And gave ourselves names
> It's me, oh, it's me
> If I am the one, who

Let out the secret
It's me, oh, it's me
May the fire burn me
It's me, oh, it's me…

When Dog tried to jump over the fire, the flames leapt into the air to kiss him by his nose, and he started to burn. Terrified, both Hen and Goat dashed to the pond

and brought back water and sand to slake the blisters. Luckily for Dog, they were so fast that the burns had not spread to other parts beyond his nose. It was clear from the turn of events Dog could not be trusted by the other two. Humiliated, Dog placed his tail between his legs and scampered down the path.

From that day onwards Dog has kept his distance from Goat and Hen, while these two animals can be seen eating at the same place and keeping each other company. And whenever they look at Dog's nose they are reminded of the importance of keeping pledges.

CROCODILE AND THE BIRDS

When God created Crocodile, he gave him beautiful, smooth skin which was the envy of many. Indeed, people came from all over to ask him how he preserved his beautiful skin, and he would pass on the secret of bathing with a loofah sponge to remove any dust caught in the pores, then greasing the skin with shea butter, coconut and palm kernel oils. He would also advise the women to cook with red palm nut oil if they must use any oil at all, because red palm nut oil digests easily and contributes to smooth skin. Crocodile was held in high esteem because he was also informed about the medicinal values of herbs and barks. Crocodile would have kept his smooth, shiny skin and the respect others had he not courted the vice of greed. Listen, gluttony and deception never got anyone very far; try to work hard for what you want and need. Let's find out how Crocodile got skin rough enough to make the bark of an old mango or neem tree look like glass.

During the last path-clearing ceremony which summoned all the citizens of the land to help weed the paths, prune the trees, unclog the gutters, sweep the market, clean the beaches and generally tidy the environment, the bird kingdom had done excellent work. The other animals were very impressed, and they decided to organize a feast in honour of the birds. Instead of the Lion's palace as venue for the event, the animals chose the top of the tree, the natural habitat of the birds. The birds were delighted at the recognition of their efforts and they got ready to attend the banquet. They called a meeting in order to discuss the modalities for the occasion.

Parrot, the leader, was the first to speak:

"My kinsmen, let's call for good health and continued success."

"May good health and success come," the others chirped in response.

"Crow," he called the attention of his linguist.

"I am here, go on," Crow accepted to mediate between the leader and the people.

"Let everybody here know that tomorrow is a very important day in our history," Parrot continued.

"Nana wants you to consider tomorrow as the most important day in your lives," Crow informed the birds. Parrot went on: "Tomorrow, at the feast, we are all going to appear in our best clothes and behaviour. I want to stress the last part: our best behaviour.

"We are a disciplined people, but you must remember that having risen above the others through our own efforts, we are bound to attract their jealousy. What it means is that others will watch us closely in order to find fault with us, even where there is none. If one of us misbehaves, we will all suffer the result. The old proverb says that when one sheep suffers from yaws the whole flock contracts the disease. I don't want to see birds so overwhelmed by the food that they rush at it and behave like hooligans. We are of royal lineage, closer to God, and that is why we live in the sky. Never forget that."

"My fellow royal birds," said Crow, "Nana wants us all to behave in a way commensurate with our social class in this kingdom. Tomorrow we are going to be honoured, and we must behave like creatures worthy of respect. I know the state of my voice, so I will keep my beak firmly clasped no matter how tempted I become to sing along with the sparrows and nightingales chosen to sing the opening hymn. If you are a glutton," and here the linguist paused to look in the direction of Vulture, "leave your excesses on the rubbish dump for the duration of the feast. If you know that you have a bad temper," this was addressed specifically to the Woodpecker, "remember that tomorrow is not the day for settling disputes. The chatterboxes (meaning the tiny, noisy nkyen birds), "please hold your beaks while the ceremony goes on, except to eat, of course! And above all, we should not forget the little ones that we shall be leaving in the nests. We should all bring home some food. This is one of our habits, to come home from a feast with food for those left at home."

When the meeting was about to end Seagull raised a point which prolonged the meeting: He suggested that since they were the ones being honoured, they should find another animal to act as spokesman between them and the other animals. The others all thought it was a good idea, so that the others would have been involved somehow. They threw up various possibilities. Monkey was dismissed because he was too haughty. Elephant? Never! Despite his huge size it was the little black ant that killed his chief. As for Kweku Ananse the Spider, you only consult him when you are tired of a peaceful life and you want calamity on your head and on the heads of countless generations to come. Tortoise? He moves so slowly that by the time he gets to the banquet site only the crumbs will tell that something happened hours before. How about Crab? But who will take Crab seriously when even the way he walks provokes such laughter? And so they dismissed each animal until someone mentioned Crocodile.

"Why did it take us so long to suggest Crocodile? With his smooth skin he will make the perfect spokesman", Partridge commented. A delegation of birds was sent to consult with Crocodile, who readily accepted to play the role of spokesman. Then came the task of getting Crocodile up the tree where the feast was supposed to take place. After some discussion the birds made up their minds to donate feathers to enable Crocodile to fly.

A group of hawks was given the task of collecting gum from the rubber tree while the sparrows arranged the feathers on Crocodile's body. Together, the birds did a splendid job and Crocodile was quite a spectacle. The birds' selection of feathers showed a vibrant and intricate use of colour, and they had so arranged them as to create an impressive pattern on their mouthpiece.

Encouraged by the other birds, Crocodile tried and succeeded at flying. He realised that it was a much easier activity than he had thought. He flew to the river, took a look at his reflection and understood why he was earning so much praise for his looks, even from Parrot.

When the great day finally dawned, the birds woke up earlier than usual, excited by the prospect of the feast. Later in the morning they all assembled, and discussed the manner of arrival at the top of the tree. It was agreed that the spokesman would go first, followed by the smaller birds while the larger ones completed the file.

By that time, the strategy forming in the mind of Crocodile took complete form; he planned to rob the birds of their reward. And so he said to the birds, "There is a problem. When the animals ask of my name, I can't tell them I am Crocodile or they'll take me for an imposter and chase me away. My new name is 'All of you,' so please remember that."

The birds saw no harm in the new name and even thanked Crocodile for thinking up such a good name for himself. When Crocodile flew in, the other animals were surprised indeed because they had never seen a bird so big or so beautiful. They took him for the god of the birds, brought out on this special day to oversee the ceremony. The others flew in and took their positions on various branches of the tree. The first dish was a plate of jollof rice cooked with chicken, mutton and beans. Donkey left the dish at the bottom of the tree, and brayed in his loud voice: "This dish is for all of you."

"Have you heard? The newly-named Crocodile asked the surprised birds, before insisting, "This food is mine, so you had better wait for yours."

He flew down and brought up the food, which he ate all by himself.

A couple of minutes later Fox brought a dish of fufu and light soup cooked with smoked mudfish, and said: "This dish is for all of you."

"Well, what can I say? This dish is mine as well, and it will be impolite of me not to eat it." Crocodile did not invite anyone to share in this meal either.

The next dish was fried plantain and bean stew, which Rat carried on his head. He left the platter at the bottom of the tree and yelled to the birds: "the food belongs to ALL OF YOU." Crocodile again enjoyed the meal to his satisfaction.

The duiker was the next to bring the dish of nkontomire stew prepared with the leaves of the cocoyam plant, pumpkin seeds and mushrooms. In another bowl were boiled yams, cocoyam and green plantain. He told the birds: "all of you must eat this food," as he left the bowls of food under the tree.

This strategy continued with the main dishes and desserts of roasted plantains, corn and groundnuts, and as well with the gourds of palm wine which the other animals brought. The birds could see that Crocodile had fooled them, but they were determined to show that they were well-mannered, by staying till the end of the feast. As soon as Lion, King of the forest, and his entourage had left, the birds rushed to Crocodile, yanked off their feathers and left him stranded. So there was Crocodile at the top of the tree, having no idea how to get down. He pleaded with the birds but they would not listen to him.

Then as a last resort he made a request, that they ask his neighbour to bring all the soft and padded items from his house; he asked for articles like clothes, the mattresses and pillows stuffed with kapok and velvet cloths. As well, Crocodile instructed, his neighbour must cut the trunks of plantain plants and beat them till they were very soft. He must bring all these objects and spread them under the tree so that Crocodile could jump down onto a cushioned surface without breaking his bones.

"Ah, Crocodile! To think we just wanted him to share in our joy, and he proceeds to make a complete laughingstock of us! What makes him think we will send the message to his neighbour? Crocodile is looking for firewood where the pawpaw tree has fallen!" Parrot candidly summed up the situation.

The birds decided that in order to have their own back on Crocodile, they would turn the message around. They found his neighbour sharpening his cutlass on a piece of stone and humming to himself. The birds told him that Crocodile had entered a bet which would transform their lives, but he needed some items.

"What does he need? Crocodile has always been wise, and I will give anything to be freed from this life of drudgery," said his neighbour, quite anxiously. The birds told him that Crocodile wanted him to bring cutlasses, stones, tall grass with sharp blade ends, nettles, firewood, broken pieces of calabash and pots, bamboo sticks, thorny bushes, knives and any other articles which can cause injury, and spread them under a particular tree. The birds even helped the neighbour carry the farm implements and other objects, which they spread on the ground under the tree. Crocodile was too high up in the tree to see exactly what those articles were, so that when his neighbour told him to jump down, he threw down his body and crashed into the items on the ground! Upon impact, he sustained all manner of cuts, bruises and scratches.

Crocodile screamed for help, his body dripping with blood. His neighbour rushed to an old woman who gave him a threaded needle to sew together the broken skin. The emergency stitches, which his neighbour used to hurriedly pull his skin together, left a very awkward pattern on Crocodile. No amount of oils ever succeeded at smoothing his skin back to its original condition.

30

KWEKU ANANSE AND THE WAILING CANE

The famine that unleashed itself on the town in which Kweku Ananse and his family lived was unprecedented in human memory. For seasons the rains had refused to fall, and no amount of fasting and sacrifices had made any difference. It has even been whispered that the people got so desperate that they had contemplated sacrificing a human being! The inhabitants of the village spent their days wandering in the forest looking for anything edible. During the famine, people had to eat whatever they could find. There was hardly any space for food preferences and choices; these are the habits that make sense in times of abundance.

It was interesting, at the beginning of the famine, to see those for whom it was a taboo to eat pork fight over salted pig feet and ears with those who had always eaten them. Those individuals who had taught themselves to dislike certain food items had to learn to eat them again, and were glad to have anything in their stomachs. Cassava dough flour, previously regarded as poor man's food, had become a rare commodity. People pawned their family heirlooms and their cloths for food. Even the gods had to be pacified with any fowl, irrespective of the colour of its feathers. And after a while, the gods had to listen to man's supplication without any animal sacrifice because there was nothing to be sacrificed.

People had lost so much weight that their ribs and collarbones stood out prominently on their bodies. The children did better because the adults always made sure that children were fed first with whatever was available. But even then, no child had enough to eat. Once, a family who was roaming in the forest had found roots that looked like cassava. They had come home, cooked and eaten them. The entire family was wiped out because the roots were highly poisonous. Only the coconut tree continued to bear fruit, but we all know that too much dried coconut is not good.

What hurt the people of this town the most was the humiliation that goes with hunger. They were not a lazy people, and they had a history of which they were extremely proud. They were used to taking good care of themselves, yet somehow, nature had dealt such an awful blow at them.

The oldest son of Kweku Ananse, called Ntikuma, was wandering in the forest one day during the famine. The sun continued to shine; the ground was hot to the foot. Ntikuma wondered what would happen if there was no rain that year. He quickly banished that thought from his mind because he could not conceive of things getting any worse than they already were. After looking under a barren

palm tree, he was fortunate enough to find three palm nuts which though edible, no one normally ate. Intending to take them home to share with his family, Ntikuma walked about and looked for two pieces of stone to crack them with.

After he placed the first palm nut on one stone and hit it with the other, the kernel jumped from between the stones and disappeared into a nearby hole. The boy frowned; he had not even noticed it was there. Moving away from the hole, he cracked the second shell open. Yet, the second kernel, too, leapt and landed in the hole. After the third and last palm kernel also found its way into the hole, Ntikuma decided to go down into that opening in search of the palm kernels.

When Ntikuma descended into the hole, he found a wide clearing, occupied by a very old woman sitting and threading beads. Ntikuma politely greeted the old woman:

"Good afternoon, my grandmother."

"Good afternoon, my grandson, what brings you here today?"

"Awo, the hunger which has struck my land has reduced us to beggars on our own soil. The distress is unimaginable. The land is desiccated and cracked; we cannot plant anything.

"We have eaten almost all the seed which we stored for planting, and we are also afraid of dying of hunger. Even children have had to learn how to stave off hunger pangs by chewing kola. This afternoon I came to see what I could find for my family, and I was very happy to collect three palm kernels. Unfortunately each of them disappeared down a hole. And so I made up my mind to come down the hole to retrieve my kernels, which is how I came here. I do not mean to disturb you. I just want to collect my palm kernels and go away."

The old woman had pity on Ntikuma. She asked him to take her walking stick and a huge basket and go in a direction she pointed out to him.

"Soon you will see a farm with all manner of vegetables and tubers. But you must listen carefully: the plants will talk to you. Ignore those who shout 'pick me, pick me!' and only harvest those who say, 'don't pick me, don't pick me!' As long as you follow these instructions, you can come here as often as you want and take away as much food as you need."

When Ntikuma got to the farm he saw such a flourishing of plants as he had not seen in a very long time. The farm reminded him once again of the various shades of green that a farm can exhibit. The old woman was right. There were so many vegetables – some he could identify and others that were not familiar to him. As he moved closer he heard the plants talking. Some had a voice with which to yell: 'pick me, pick me!' while others screamed: 'don't pick me, don't pick me!'

Ntikuma was careful to avoid those who wanted to be picked and only harvest those who did not want to be selected. In this way he gathered tomatoes, eggplants, peppers, cocoyam leaves, beans, oranges and papaws. He also cut a bunch each of bananas and plantains and uprooted yams, cocoyam and sweet potatoes. He arranged the food carefully in the basket and brought them before the old woman, Awo. She told Ntikuma to leave her walking stick and go home. Awo went on to assure Ntikuma that he could come again if they ran out of food, adding, "Very soon there will be rainfall in your land."

When Ntikuma got home, his father, mother and brothers were sleeping. The idea was that they would conserve their energy by sleeping most of the time and take turns looking for food. Moreover, sleeping made them forget their hunger. Ntikuma woke them up to come and see what he had brought. His family was utterly surprised. His mother, Aso, could not recall the last time she had seen such fresh vegetables and of such variety. She decided that they would cook the food and invite everyone to share in it, since the famine had spared no one. Kweku Ananse strongly disagreed. He wanted them to keep the food to themselves. Not even Ntikuma's explanation that he could bring the same amount of food each day made Ananse change his mind. However, Aso was determined to share the food with the neighbours. This she did, much to the anger of her husband.

Ntikuma continued to bring food to the entire community, which started to laugh again. The inhabitants of the town started calling Ntikuma Ɔsaagyefo the saviour, Ɔyaadeɛyie the one who puts everything right and so many other names to show their appreciation for the role he played in bringing an end to the famine even though it had still not rained. And in fact, the town would have continued to experience bliss had it not been for the greed of Kweku Ananse the spider.

Kweku Ananse reasoned that it would be so much better if he also knew the secret to the abundant food. Unlike his son Ntikuma who willingly shared what he had, Kweku Ananse wanted two things out of the endeavour: The first was to acquire the same respect his son had. He had been feeling jealous of the popularity of his son since his discovery of the food. When he overheard a discussion about making Ntikuma Saanaahene so he would take charge of the King's treasury, Ananse felt it was time to show his son and everyone that it was he who had fathered the boy. The second reason he wanted to discover where Ntikuma brought the food from was that it would give Ananse the chance to get his own back on his wife Aso who had dared to disagree with him. This way, he could finally use the food as he saw fit.

Ananse pestered his son until Ntikuma revealed the food source to his father. Ntikuma felt that he was doing the right thing because Awo had never told him not to divulge the information.

Early the next morning Kweku Ananse set off for the site of the palm tree. He had no difficulty finding it. He had gone with his own palm kernels, though most people had thrown theirs away at the end of

the famine. Ananse cracked the kernels with unnecessary force, to propel them away from him. Yet the nuts stayed intact and did not move an inch. Certainly this did not please Ananse so he found the hole and pushed the nuts through. After the third one had gone down the hole, Ananse followed suit.

Just as his son had described, Ananse saw an old woman. He however addressed her with disrespect: "Hey, old woman, what are you doing still alive? You are the classic case of the withered leaf which remains on the tree while the green, young one, is cut off. Anyway, I am hungry."

The old woman was very calm and replied:

"My name is Awo. I am still alive because the ancestors have not called me yet, and I am supposed to help end the famine. You must listen carefully: take my walking stick and this basket and walk towards my farm. You must ignore the plants which say 'pick me, pick me!' and rather, pick those who say, 'don't pick me, don't pick me!'"

"Ei, old woman, you must be a bad witch. How else did you come to plant talking vegetables? No wonder you are alone here. Besides, you are so old that you have lost your common sense. Why should I pick food items which want to enjoy living and spare those who have had enough of life and want to die? But there is no point in arguing with you."

Ananse snatched the walking stick and basket and hurried to the farm. He found it hard to determine what impressed him most, whether it was the freshness of the vegetables or their ability to talk. When the plants started to say 'pick me, pick me!' Kweku Ananse told them their wish would be granted, and he filled his basket with those kinds of produce. To those who said: 'don't pick me, don't pick me!', Ananse told them not to worry because he was not as stupid as that demented old woman they had for a caretaker with her brains all turned upside down. He also told them to continue to enjoy life.

Ananse decided that the walking stick looked too good for the old woman, so he would keep it for himself. When Awo asked for her stick, Ananse struck her with it so hard that the force of it sent her reeling to the floor, dead.

Ananse felt that the death of Awo would automatically transfer ownership of the farm to him, and even Ntikuma and the powerful kingmakers would have to come and in all humility, beg him for food. Then, Ananse mused, the elders would have a fine context for the selection of the Sanaahene, the king's treasurer. It was a victorious Ananse who entered the town and who declared with confidence that the path to everyone's stomach passed through his domain. He carefully

put away the food and decided to exchange it for gold, diamonds, kente cloths and precious beads.

Unfortunately for Ananse, that day announced the end of the famine. It began with a drizzle. The inhabitants of the town were so excited that both children and adults stood in the rain until their clothes got wet. The next three days caught the fever, and the showers fell uninhibited. The ground was soaked and some plants even started to sprout. Ananse consoled himself by saying that with his free farm, there was no point in joining the others to plant. Ananse had to eat the food all alone because the people refused to exchange the little wealth they had left for food. It was clear to the farmers that they could plant some fast-growing vegetables and end the hunger.

Ananse forced himself again down the hole to pick the vegetables which asked to be picked. However, just as he got ready to put the basket on his head, the walking stick turned into a whipping cane and started to whip Ananse, while it sang a dirge for Awo. Ananse threw away the basket of food and ran for his life, but the rod would not leave him alone. It followed him out of the hole to his house, pursued by passers-by who found the phenomenon odd indeed.

Most of the people were happy and jeered openly at the agony of greedy Ananse. Ntikuma was the only one who could figure out how to calm the stick. When some people told him what was going on in his house Ntikuma decided to take his time with his farm work, in order to allow Ananse to enjoy his communion with the wailing cane a little longer. Meanwhile, the cane gave Ananse no respite, and those who took pity on him and tried to save him were whipped too. When Ntikuma came from the farm and saw that his father had suffered enough, he led him to the hole and made him go down and pick the vegetables and fruits according to the directives of Awo. Only then did the cane stop whipping Ananse and fall to the ground.

When Ananse came back to the village, he was so ashamed that he took one look to his left, another to his right and jumped to the roof of his house, from where he has been hanging since.

WHY THE HIPPOPOTAMUS LIVES IN WATER

Today, the hippopotamus, like the crocodile and the fish, lives in water. A long time ago the hippopotamus lived on land like the fox, the tiger, the monkey, the lion and the other animals that still live in the forest. In this same forest lived Kweku Ananse the spider. Ananse was revered in the forest by all the animals because, despite his delicate frame, he was endowed with cunning which he always employed to maximum effect. Of course there were a number of times when his greed got the better of him, but generally speaking, Ananse was a clever fellow.

One cool afternoon, Ananse went to visit Hippopotamus, who lived in a nearby village. Hippopotamus was happy to receive Ananse into his house, but he knew that the spider was full of tricks and sometimes, roguery. The two exchanged greetings and made enquiries about the health of their families. Satisfied that no major problem had brought Ananse to his house, Hippopotamus brought out a gourd of palm wine which he had tapped only that morning. Ananse was delighted by the drink, and the two drank as they discussed matters of mutual concern. The subject of their conversation roved from the problems of marriage, of raising children, the changing weather and the relationships between the animals, to the subject of power- specifically, physical energy. The two of them agreed on all the issues they raised, except on the issue of power.

Kweku Ananse insisted that he should be included in the list of strong animals, but Hippopotamus disagreed. He came close to reminding Ananse of his skinny legs, tiny waist and fragile system, but he felt that such words might change the mood of the discussion for the worse. So just for a moment imagine how Hippopotamus felt when Ananse challenged him to a tug of war!! Hippopotamus laughed until tears rolled off his cheeks. And yet, Ananse was dead serious.

"I know what I am talking about, and please do not blame it on the palm wine. I am not drunk."

"Oh, yes, the drunkards are always quick to tell everyone that they are sober. But Ananse, seriously, how can you compare your strength to mine? Are you sure about what you are getting yourself into?"

His eyes flashing with intrigue and with scorn in his voice, Ananse replied:

"There are two things that are very clear to me: I am very conscious of my figure, and I also know for sure that I can challenge the entire range of so-called strong animals in the forest to a tug of war and win."

"So, you can win against Horse!"

"Who is there to stop me?"

"And against Elephant!"

"With my eyes closed."

"And against Leopard!"

"Hands down."

"How about Lion?

"With one hand tied to my back."

"Ei, Kweku Ananse... and can you win a tug of war against Whale?"

"Do you have a reason why I should not?"

"So you are sure to win a tug of war against me!"

"And why not?"

Hippopotamus was then convinced that Ananse was determined to challenge him. He was very insulted when Ananse told him that he felt Hippopotamus needed time to prepare for the tug of war, so he should set the date and inform him because *he* was ready any day. The strides that took Ananse out of the house of Hippopotamus exuded nothing but confidence, while Hippopotamus' face clearly showed how aggrieved he felt.

From Hippopotamus' house, Ananse went to the house of Elephant, who was mending his roof. Elephant stopped work and came to sit by Ananse. The conversation turned immediately sour when Ananse declared that he could challenge Elephant to a tug of war. Elephant lost his temper immediately and rushed to give Ananse a slap.

The latter was quick to escape to the roof and tell Elephant that he meant a tug of war, and neither wrestling nor boxing. Still fuming, Elephant suggested to Ananse that the contest should take place immediately. When Ananse asked Elephant for the ropes, Elephant realised that they needed more time to prepare for the tournament. They agreed to postpone the contest to the following week when they would have cut enough strong creepers and they would have made the necessary ropes. When Ananse got home his wife gave him the message that Hippopotamus had sent word that the contest would be held during the following week. Ananse was delighted.

On the day of the match, Ananse told his wife, as he left home, that there was a duel between Elephant and Hippopotamus, and that he was to be the judge. Ananse had meanwhile made some very strong ropes which he had carried with a lot of difficulty to the houses of Elephant and Hippopotamus, who lived about a hundred yards away from each other.

He headed first for the house of Hippopotamus, whom he found sitting under the awning of his porch, ready to enjoy a meal of boiled yams and smoked meat. He asked Ananse to proceed immediately, so that the contest would be over and he could enjoy his meal without any insolent animal casting aspersions on his strength. Careful to avoid an argument, Ananse tied one end of the rope to Hippopotamus' chest. Hippopotamus watched Ananse as he panted over this job, and wondered why Ananse had no sense of limits.

When the job was done, Ananse told Hippopotamus that he would tie the other end to his own waist, move to a distance and shout, 'start pulling'. That should be the signal for the competition to begin. Hippopotamus just nodded in response, highly indignant at Ananse and his unrestrained self-confidence.

After tying the rope to Hippopotamus, Ananse went to Elephant's house and found him ready for the contest. Elephant had roasted plantains and groundnuts to celebrate his victory which he

knew was not in doubt. When Ananse suggested tying the end of the rope to his waist, Elephant replied that he would save Ananse the ordeal of going round his waist, and suggested that he simply tie the rope to his leg. So, this is how Kweku Ananse managed to tie one end of the rope to Hippopotamus, and the other end to Elephant.

Before he went away he told Elephant that he was going to tie the other end of the rope to his own waist and when he heard, 'start pulling', it meant the beginning of the game.

Exhausted after tying the ropes, Kweku Ananse went and sat under the shade of an avocado tree which stood between the houses of the two unwitting competitors. The rope which connected the waist of one to the leg of the other ran right in front of the avocado tree. Ananse drank some water which he had left in a gourd. He also plucked a couple of ripe fruits which he started to eat. When he was adequately refreshed and nourished, he leaned against the tree in order to relax better, and shouted, 'start pulling!'

At first, neither animal made any effort at all to move, waiting for Ananse to exhaust himself. Then Hippopotamus decided to bring the comedy to an end by pulling. Elephant was surprised to feel the tug at his leg, and he also put in some effort.

Hippopotamus could hardly believe that such energy could come from Ananse, and that was when he started to take the contest seriously. The match gathered momentum, with both animals pulling with all their energy and sweating profusely. Although Elephant's foot hurt sorely and the rope had left a bruise around Hippopotamus' waist, they could not bring themselves to give up. How would they narrate the manner of their defeat? That Kweku Ananse had won a tug-of-war against them? Impossible! So, this contest lasted throughout the day. Elephant had stopped glancing at his roasted plantains and groundnuts which had gone awfully cold, while Hippopotamus watched a swarm of flies feast on his smoked meat and boiled yams. As for Kweku Ananse, he would refresh himself with avocado fruit and water as he watched the two animals pull at the strong ropes.

Finally, the rope snapped, much to the consternation of both Hippopotamus and Elephant. It meant that neither side had won, and even more disturbing, that Ananse was a strong animal indeed. Elephant was so upset by the turn of events that he decided to go straight to the house of his friend Hippopotamus and tell him what had happened. How could he summon the energy and the will to face

another monstrous battle with Kweku Ananse, a mere spider? Arrived at the house of Hippopotamus, Elephant saw his friend lying on the ground, too weak to move. When Elephant approached him and found the rope at his waist, and when at the same time, Hippopotamus found a piece of the same rope around the foot of his friend, both knew at once that Kweku Ananse had played a practical joke on them.

In order to avoid impending humiliation, Elephant suggested one of them should move away from land, while the other paid occasional visits. Hippopotamus volunteered to move as far away from Ananse as possible, by moving into the nearby river and living in water. Elephant would spend time with his friend whenever possible, away from any prying eyes.

As for Kweku Ananse, he was counted among the mentally strong in all the land.

THE CAT AND HIS CHANGING ALLEGIANCES

Sometime ago, Cat lived in the forest with all manner of wild animals. Cat was not a strong animal and so he liked to make friends with the animal he believed could protect him the best. The first friend he had was Antelope, whom he liked and respected very much.

Antelope would share his catch with his friend, and one day he saved Cat from the trap which Tortoise had set just for him. Cat really appreciated the kindness of Antelope and determined after his escape from death never to leave his company.

One day when the sun had spent its energy for the day and was making way for the moon, the two friends strolled towards the pond to drink water. What they did not know was that Lion had been watching Antelope develop strong muscles; he could tell from the weight Antelope had gained that he would make a tasty meal.

Lion decided the day had come for him to kill Antelope. He met the two animals coming from the pond and he greeted them:

"Good evening, Antelope and Cat." After the others responded, Lion asked:

"Antelope, I am glad I have met you today. In fact, I have been looking for you for a while. Can you explain why you have planned to court my wife?" Antelope was so taken aback that he stared at Cat, then at Lion then back at Cat. He took a close look at his surroundings to make sure that he was not dreaming, before he could collect his thoughts in order to give an answer:

"King of the forest, Lion, what kind of trouble do you want to draw me into? I don't even know your wife. In fact I have never seen her since my mother gave birth to me. Besides, I am not aware of Antelopes who court female lions. Who told you such a damaging piece of news?" Antelope was indeed very surprised. As for Cat he was shivering with fright, not knowing what to think.

"Exactly! My informant told me that the first thing you would do would be to deny it. I have confronted my wife with the charge and she has already confessed that you have been sending her gifts; she has also told me where and when the two of you meet. Why do you want to make a laughingstock of the king of the forest?" Antelope replied that Lion's wife was not part of his thoughts either by day or by night.

When Lion went on to accuse Antelope of impregnating his wife, Antelope thought that was the limit:

"You must be mad! Have you heard, since the Sky God created seven days, of an antelope and a lion having babies together?"

"Oh! Now I have come to understand your actions. Apart from seducing my wife you have the insolence to call me mad! I will show you that I am mad indeed." With these words Lion pounced on Antelope and killed him with one deadly blow. He then dragged the corpse to his wife who smoked the meat and cooked the evening meal with it.

While Lion was leaving the scene, Cat followed him to his home. Cat figured that if Lion could so easily kill Antelope, then he was better off living with Lion because he was stronger than Antelope and Lion could give him better protection. At first he was afraid of Lion, but after he had lived with him and his family for a few seasons, he saw a side of lions that the stories somehow always omitted; not that Lion did a good job showing this sensitive side by this encounter with Antelope. Lion and his family appeared to be very gentle and loving. Cat could not have imagined for his life that lions had a sense of humour, or that they could be so sensitive.

The lion family accepted Cat into their fold and shared their food with him. Cat felt secure, and he would even accompany Lion on his hunting trips.

Cat would normally hide behind a tree or some bushes while Lion stalked and eventually killed his victims, because, as I have already told you, Cat was spineless. Lion liked the idea of proving his strength to someone as cowardly as Cat. For the benefit of his timid friend and for his own gratification, Lion would make a great show of tact and energy as he killed even animals like hares which he would normally get rid of without much ado. Cat really came to admire and respect both the mastery and aptitude of Lion. Even though he sometimes missed Antelope, Cat became convinced that he had somehow gained something from his death as he witnessed more and more of Lion's accomplishments.

One day while they went out hunting, Lion and Cat saw a huge figure moving towards them. It was no other animal than Elephant. Lion greeted Elephant and as he passed by him, but Elephant stopped Lion in his course with his trunk and declared:

"Lion, you call yourself 'king of the forest' and for a long time the animals have all believed it and they give you more respect than me."

Lion was surprised that Elephant would make a case out of an established truth. When he started to laugh by way of responding, Elephant was really outraged. Lion answered him:

"Look, Elephant, this comment is strange indeed. Do you know something — I was not the one who gave myself that noble title. I don't know how things are done in your tribe, but in mine we don't drum our own praises. We leave it to the talking drummer and praise singer who represent knowledge to do so. I have heard that in the tribe of the jackasses things are changing so fast that those who have a lot of wealth buy titles while others appropriate them through the use of force. They should consider that their decisions affect several generations to come.

"If I have earned such an appellation it is because I have achievements which support the description. I think you should learn a little bit more about how thinking creatures obtain their appellations before you confront them with false claims."

While all of this exchange was going on Cat was, as usual, hiding in the branches of a tree he had hastily climbed. He was afraid, but at the same time he enjoyed the drama. He remembered how Lion had falsely indicted his benefactor the antelope in order to enjoy his meat. Meanwhile the two great beasts continued with their altercation: "Move your massive body away from the path so that I can get on with my business, unless you are tired of living," Lion said loftily.

No sooner were these words out of the mouth of Lion than Elephant simply draped his immense body on Lion.

When he got up a short while later, Lion lay flat like a crushed sugarcane stick, dead. As Elephant walked away with a sense of achievement, Cat made up his mind that from that time onwards he would always stick by the Elephant because he was even stronger than the king of the forest.

Life with Elephant proved exciting but different. Cat found that Elephant fed mostly on vegetables, but he was no farmer. All Elephant needed to do was to enter any farm and eat as much as he wanted to. What Cat liked so much was the havoc which Elephant regularly caused in his trail. He could destroy farms by stepping on the plants, and remove whole trees simply by twirling his trunk around them and pulling as he walked away.

At one time when Elephant decided to divert himself by going to a village and destroying the houses and crops, Cat came to understand why Elephant would feel offended that he was not called 'king of the forest.' After this particular incident Cat told Elephant that he should be called both 'king of the forest' and 'king of the village.' Elephant was delighted. He was not aware that the citizens of the same village had planned to kill him. The hunter had in fact been tracking Elephant for a long time, and when he found him, he killed him at once with a single shot from his gun.

"Goodness", Cat exclaimed as he followed the hunter home. "So there is someone stronger than Elephant! What kind of stick did he use? It is a strange stick which lets out smoke and a loud noise. From now on, I will be friends only with this person." When the hunter announced that he had killed the menacing elephant, the villagers were beside themselves with gratitude and admiration. Cat thus stayed close to the household of the hunter and his wife. The hunter's wife was a cane-basket weaver.

"Who is this animal?" She asked the hunter.

"I don't know his name, but he has been following me since I shot the elephant," he replied. "He appears to be harmless, and he may be useful around the house. The last time I saw him kill the mice who have been feeding on the corn we grow, and he was actually the one who overpowered that brown snake until I came with my gun and finished off the venomous reptile."

"That being the case we must keep him and feed him", suggested the hunter's wife.

Cat had a peaceful life with the hunter and the basket weaver who treated him most kindly. He also made himself useful by catching the cockroaches and the mice and keeping the snakes at bay. Cat felt that there was no creature stronger than the hunter because he could kill any animal he chose with his smoking stick.

One afternoon while the sun was blazing and people rested under the shade of trees, Cat heard a heated argument between the hunter and his wife the basket weaver. He could not tell the exact cause of the quarrel, but it was obvious from their tones that something had gone wrong. Before the other residents could intervene, out rushed the powerful hunter screaming for help! His wife was chasing him, holding a couple of the canes she used to weave her baskets in one hand and a pestle in the other!! The villagers laughed at the hunter's predicament. Cat watched as this brawny, powerful and respected man was reduced to a whimpering child hollering for help.

"So," Cat mused, "Hunter who can kill even an elephant and order his wife about at times cannot withstand a small weapon like a cane and a pestle! It must be because woman holds those weapons. The power of Woman must be more formidable than that of Lion, Elephant and Hunter. Its potency must be the reason it shows itself rarely. From now on I will stay close to Woman. She must be the most forceful being in the world."

To this day, Cat stays close to the hearth. He likes to keep women company and rub his body against theirs as tribute to the magical powers of women.

KWEKU ANANSE AND HIS FIVE WIVES

Kweku Ananse's neighbour, Odasanyi, was a very rich man. Odasanyi owned cocoa, kola, groundnut, bean and corn farms. He had an animal farm too, in which you would see turkeys, chicken, ducks, pheasants, pigs, goats, rams, sheep, cows and rabbits. Odasanyi traded in cash crops with people of other lands who could not grow the same. Kweku Ananse, on the other hand, owned just a few stalks of corn, a small vegetable patch and no domestic animals. But Odasanyi liked to share with his friend, and so Kweku Ananse never lacked meat with his meals. However, this good relationship did not last long because Odasanyi did not have his wits about him at all times and because greed took over the mind of Kweku Ananse.

What both Odasanyi and Ananse had in common was that they were both bachelors, and although his marital status hardly bothered Ananse, Odasanyi wanted to get married. He went over to the house of Ananse one evening and discussed the matter with his friend. Odasanyi regretted that should he die soon there would be no close relation of his to take over his business and make it grow. Moreover, he went on, he felt really lonely, having neither wife nor children.

From the experience he had with the children of his trading partners and distant relatives, he knew that no love was purer than the love of a child – children love without counting the cost. Odasanyi did not want to have children with women he was not married to, as Ananse had suggested. Odasanyi's idea of parenthood included living with the child and its mother, and the family showing concern for each other.

Kweku Ananse then also decided that it was a good idea to think of getting married, He also went on that he wanted to get married too, because he was tired of eating the "bachelors' soup" for which he was becoming famous. He wanted a woman to help him on his farm and if he played his cards well he could marry two or three women who would compete with each other over his affection as some women were wont to do; he would just sit back and enjoy the fruits of that competition. While Odasanyi did not want to have to deal with the tensions of polygamy because he thought there would be enough to keep him busy with one woman, Ananse saw no reason to abandon a marriage arrangement that stood to work in his favour. They both agreed, however, to set off the following day to the next village, noted for their industrious and beautiful women, in search of wives.

When the two of them met at the appointed time, Ananse wore a patched pair of shorts and a shirt which had paid too many visits to the laundry. He wore no sandals on his feet because he owned none. Odasanyi on the other hand, wore a pair of velvet shorts over which he had thrown his exquisite kente cloth. He had a couple of rings on his finger and a heavy gold chain with a pendant shaped like a stool. On his feet he wore a pair of black slippers, the kind which only royalty wore in the olden days.

Ananse saw immediately that he stood very little chance of convincing the family of any woman of his worthiness, given the way he looked. He quickly thought of a plan. He told Odasanyi that since he wanted to marry only one woman and since he was so rich, he would have to be careful not to be hooked to a woman who would fall only for his money. Such women, Ananse went on, had ways of killing their

husbands in order to enjoy their wealth with the man that they really wanted. Ananse narrated a few such horror stories with such conviction that Odasanyi got scared. That was exactly the mood Ananse was waiting for.

He told his friend that since he was already poor, he needed the appearance of wealth in order to attract mates, and then when the brides came to his home and found how poorly he lived, they would stay if the women were driven by true love. In like manner, Ananse convinced Odasanyi that the woman who felt attracted to

79

him despite the appearance of poverty would love him all the better if she found out that he were rich. Odasanyi fell for the trick and quickly exchanged his clothes for those of Ananse.

The two friends arrived at the market place where a lot of the single women traded. Many of them were attracted by the rich clothes that Ananse wore, and they shunned Odasanyi who appeared like a beggar who had lost his way. When one curious young woman started talking to Odasanyi the other shrieked at her, asking what she wanted to do with a tramp.

But the more she talked to him, the more she found how intelligent and warm Odasanyi was. The young woman, Maanan, was impressed by Odasanyi's mind, and when he proposed to her, she accepted the offer. Meanwhile, Ananse was having a hard time choosing between the women who were flinging themselves in his path. He finally selected five women. He looked at their build and decided that they would be an asset to his farm.

The two men and their brides journeyed homeward, and just before they reached the town where their husbands lived, the wives of Ananse were quick to

spot a huge mansion which they immediately knew would be their home. The first disappointment came when contrary to their expectations, Odasanyi and his bride took the well paved road that led to that beautiful mansion, while they had to walk a couple of miles farther down a muddy, weedy path to two small huts which Ananse described as his home. The women then understood the import of the folktale which tells of a beautiful young woman who was attracted by the gloss and the outward trappings of wealth of a young man, who in reality created a miserable married life.

Maanan lived in an attractive house with a tastefully decorated interior. More than that, her husband was a sensitive, considerate, warm and attractive man who had enough confidence in himself not to begrudge his wife of her own talents. This young woman took over the running of the animal farm and she executed her tasks with such efficiency that their wealth grew in leaps and bounds.

Although he was aware that Ananse had tried to make a fool of him, the plan had worked in his favour, and Odasanyi continued to be generous with Ananse and his wives. He would send them eggs, meat, and even cloth, sometimes. However, this was a gesture which only fuelled the discontent in the hearts of the wives of Ananse, and which reminded Ananse of his own inadequacy in providing for them. His wives never wasted any time in reminding him of how he had deceived them and reduced them from the status of women who were capable of trading and looking after themselves to the level of parasites. Ananse knew no peace in his home, and so he looked for a way to get rid of Odasanyi and his wife.

Ananse went to his vegetable plot and plucked all the ripe bananas he could find – not many, mind you. Then he peeled the fruits and in the night, he went to Odasanyi's house and lined the steps that led from his bedroom with the slippery banana peel. At the bottom of the steps he placed broken bottles, calabashes and a pile of thorny, dried bushes. After this was done, Kweku Ananse raised a wail which brought his friend to the window. When Odasanyi anxiously asked what the problem was, Ananse told him in a lamentable voice that something awful had happened in his home and he needed to talk to someone.

As Odasanyi rushed down the steps to come to the aid of his friend, he tripped and hit his head against the concrete banister. The rich, generous man fell down dead on the pieces of sharp objects. After Maanan had waited for a long while, thinking that Ananse needed some privacy with his friend, she called out to him, and Ananse replied immediately that her husband wanted him to come and offer her opinion on his problem. She tied her cloth to her chest and came down the stairs. Sadly, she met the same fate as her husband's.

In anticipation of their deaths, Ananse had dug a grave a couple of yards away, into which he placed the couple. He went home and ignoring the taunts and nagging of his wives, he slept soundly. The following day he called his wives to a meeting. That was not easy, because they were fast losing all respect for him. The others finally listened to the oldest among them, Adoma, and went to find out the purpose of the meeting. Ananse informed them that Odasanyi and his wife had moved to another part of the land where he had an even bigger estate and bigger farms. As a token of their lifelong friendship, Odasanyi had asked him to move with his wives into his mansion and manage the farms like their own. The women were excited about the prospect of leisure, and they moved with impatience out of the hovels into which they had been crowded. They were convinced that Odasanyi must be the wealthiest man in the world, to have travelled without even emptying his trunks of their fine cloth and jewellery. Maanan had left behind all her belongings too.

For the first few weeks Ananse lived in a peaceful home, with all five wives quite happy. This happiness did not last, as we shall soon see. It was the ghost of Maanan which kept appearing to each wife in a dream, narrating what had actually happened. The five wives of Kweku Ananse decided it was time the scoundrel learnt a lesson. First, they disputed constantly among themselves who should do the cooking for their husband, without ever deciding who should do it. Ananse was starving in the midst of plenty! When he took to cooking for himself the women spread the image around town of the husband of five women who was starving and dying from neglect, as the proverb describes the polygamous husband. Ananse was too embarrassed to show his face in public, having become a laughingstock.

When Kweku Ananse felt that he could no longer tolerate the insults and harangue from his own wives, he decided to go to their village and divorce them all. The women could not have been happier. During the divorce proceedings, Ananse stated his case. Adoma, who was the spokesperson for the rest, stood up boldly and charged Ananse with murder, to the utter shock of the entire assembly, including Ananse who was looking forward to enjoying the wealth of Odasanyi all by himself. Armed with the information which the ghost of Maanan had provided, the elders were led to the grave, where proper burial and funeral rites were observed for the two kind people.

What happened to Kweku Ananse? I know you would like to know. When the charge of murder was laid and his oldest wife narrated the whole episode just like Maanan had described it, Kweku Ananse was so overwhelmed that he could not even deny it. He just stared right ahead of him, paralysed with guilt. At the suggestion of an elder that Ananse be killed in order to appease the dead, Ananse jumped into the rafters from where he is hanging even as I complete this story.

HOW BAT ENDED UP WITH SUCH SMALL EARS

Bat used to have large, beautiful ears, but today his ears are among the smallest in the animal kingdom, and this story will explain how that came to be.

Once upon a time, there lived a young woman called Aba who got married and moved very far away from her parents to live in her husband's town. Aba never paid a visit to her parents, nor did she show any interest in the development and events in her own village. To make things worse she made no provision to pay her family dues. Her mother and father paid her dues until they grew too old and the larger family exempted them from payment. Aba did not even turn her eyes towards the road that led to her own hometown, and thus cut herself off from everyone in her own family. It was strange behaviour indeed because we all know that no matter for how long you are married to a man, and however many children you have by him, you forever remain a member of your own family, among whom you are buried when you die.

Aba consciously separated herself from her family because she felt they were too demanding and poked their noses too deeply into her life. Her mother, for example, wanted to know everything about her husband: if he gave her enough money for food and how many pieces of cloth he gave her in a year. What annoyed Aba was that once her mother had actually commented to the hearing of Aba's husband, on how faded her daughter's cloths looked. And her father? He would speak in proverbs which told of his contempt for his son-in-law, and to confirm his suspicions right at the beginning that the young man was lazy. His favourite proverb whenever Aba's mother started to pick on her son-in-law was: you can always tell how exciting the game will be by its manner of beginning. But her grandmother! Her grandmother was the worst of them all. "Why," she would ask, "should any woman work so hard when she has a husband?" Instead of selling only vegetables like a good woman, her grandmother would carry on by resorting to the use of a proverb, Aba wanted to sell gunpowder, contrary to all expectations.

Aba loved her family but she could not stand their interference. Unfortunately for her, however, her husband's people among whom she had chosen to live were no better. In fact they were much worse because they were spiteful, resentful and ungrateful. Although it was clear to everyone who cared to see that Aba was ingenious and independent, her in-laws concluded anyway that their son was not able to support them, as was expected of him, because she was greedy and squandered his property.

This attitude particularly angered Aba because she knew, as did her husband, of her major contributions to whatever they had acquired.

She remembers when her mother-in-law came to visit at a time when she was sick. Despite her ill health, Aba went to a lot of trouble to make her mother in-law happy because the old woman's health was not very good either. One evening after she had cooked the older woman's favourite food of boiled yam and garden egg stew, she called her politely to come and eat. Can you believe how the old woman responded? She turned and asked how many times a day they eat in their house and if they were laying the insurance for their old age in their stomachs! Aba was extremely offended, but she had to swallow her emotions.

What made things worse was that a good friend of theirs was visiting and so he heard it all. And her husband? He was sitting right there, too embarrassed to make any comment.

One day Aba went to the farm to work. While she was busy weeding in between the cassava and cocoyam plants, a bird flew right above her head and caught her attention. After that it went to perch on a tree close by and started singing:

94

Aba's mother is dead, she doesn't know.

Aba's father is dead, she hasn't heard it.

Aba's grandmother is dead, she doesn't know.

When the guns went pow! pow! pow!

She never heard them.

When the talking drums sounded ken! ken! ken!

She never heard them.

When the women wailed buee! buee! buee!

She never heard them.

When her body is brought home some day,

No one will mourn her.

For no one knows Aba.

Aba turned to listen to the bird for a while but she could make no sense out of its song, and so she continued to work. The bird sang even more loudly:

Aba's mother is dead, she doesn't know.

Aba's father is dead, she hasn't heard it.

Aba's grandmother is dead, she doesn't know.

When the guns went pow! pow! pow!

She never heard them.

When the talking drums sounded ken!ken!ken!

She never heard them.

When the women wailed buee! buee! buee!

She never heard them.

When her body is brought home some day,

No one will mourn her.

For no one knows Aba.

The bird sang continuously until after a while Aba got irritated and drove it away. Yet, shortly afterwards, the bird was back on the tree and resumed singing the same song. After she had harvested many of her vegetables Aba found she could not concentrate anymore on her farm work and so she resolved to go home. The bird followed Aba all the way home and not once did it even pause for breath; it sang the same song without respite.

When she got home, she told her husband:

"I was working on the farm when a bird came and perched on the palm tree and began to sing a strange song with my name in it. At first I paid it no heed but it kept singing with such intensity that I could not give enough attention to my work. I almost cut my toe with the hoe, and that was when I decided to come home.

Even then, this bird will not leave me alone. In fact it has followed me home and is perched on the orange tree just outside the kitchen."

Aba's husband went to take a look at this bird who began to sing the same song again. After listening for a while, he went to call his parents to come and find out what calamity their daughter-in-law had brought upon them all. They all trooped to see what was going on. As soon as the bird saw them, it began to sing:

Aba's mother is dead, she doesn't know.

Aba's father is dead, she hasn't heard it.

Aba's grandmother is dead, she doesn't know.

When the guns went pow! pow! pow!

She never heard them.

When the talking drums sounded ken! ken! ken!

She never heard them.

When the women wailed buee! buee! buee!

She never heard them.

When her body is brought home some day,

No one will mourn her.

For no one knows Aba.

Many people gathered under the tree, but no one could make sense of the bird's song. The medicine man advised that the bat be called because he was reputed to be able to interpret strange messages. When Bat arrived, he made Aba narrate the whole story. As soon as she finished the narration the bird started to sing:

Aba's mother is dead, she doesn't know.

Aba's father is dead, she hasn't heard it.

Aba's grandmother is dead, she doesn't know.

When the guns went pow! pow! pow!

She never heard them.

When the talking drums sounded ken! ken! ken!

She never heard them.

When the women wailed buee! buee! buee!

She never heard them.

When her body is brought home some day,

No one will mourn her.

For no one knows Aba.

Bat gave a big sigh when the bird finished the song and he asked for a drink of gin. The request made people worried indeed because it meant that the news was bad. When the drink was brought Bat first poured libation, and then he spoke:

"Aba, this bird is carrying a message from the spirits of your mother, father and grandmother who are all dead. You never heard the sad news. The spirits are saying through the bird that when the gunshots were fired and the talking drums announced their deaths you were too far away to hear of the events. And when the women wailed loud enough to wake the dead you were again too far away to hear them. The spirits are warning you that you should not continue to cut your roots off from where your umbilical cord is now buried. They conclude that if you do not find your feet home soon, when it is your turn to be buried among your people you will hardly have any mourners from your home town because you never visit and hardly anyone will remember you. This is your message, Aba."

After the bat had so interpreted the song the bird flew away while Aba threw herself on the ground and started to weep uncontrollably. She wept so much that even her mother-in-law wept with her, while everyone tried to console Aba who refused to be pacified. Her husband tried all he could but his wife was heartbroken indeed.

She wept for various reasons, including missing even the interference of her family because although she still did not approve of their methods, maturity and experience had taught her that they meant well, and that no one cared for her better. She wept all afternoon until she her eyes got so swollen you could hardly see her eyelashes. But she had learnt her lesson the hard way. She regretted abandoning her people and she started making plans to go to her home town to establish contact with her cousins, aunts, uncles and neighbours.

The people who had come to find out the meaning of the bird's song were very impressed by Bat. They were convinced that Bat's ears were truly useful in understanding hidden messages. Each person rushed off to break a piece of Bat's ears and attach it to his or her own ear, so that their hearing would be sharper and their understanding deepened.

So this is how Bat's ears got reduced from a large, flappy size to tiny ones.

HOW KWEKU ANANSE BECAME FAMOUS

A long time ago, Kweku Ananse was an ordinary servant to a very famous and rich king. He went about his duties of tidying the rooms of the palace and generally making himself useful. There was nothing extraordinary about him, except that for some reason the wife of the king trusted Ananse absolutely. She even gave him the key to her treasury box, and there was no cause for her to be alarmed, because Ananse took good care of her jewellery and other valuable items.

One of Ananse's peculiar duties was to carry a certain covered dish to the dining table of the royal couple, and he was under strict orders never to open the dish. Ananse obeyed the instructions for many years. There were times when his curiosity would almost get the better of him and he would come close to opening the dish - but for a long time he did not dare break the rule. Ananse was able to refrain from looking inside the dish until one day, unable to resist the temptation any more, he took the dish to the inner courtyard when everyone else had gone to the farm, and took a peek. He was not prepared for what he saw! A cooked python!! Ananse almost screamed, but he collected himself and covered the surprising dish immediately.

Then after a short while, seeing that the royal couple was still receiving guests in the outer courtyard, he opened the dish again, and he saw that pieces of the snake meat had been eaten and that some leftovers lay in the dish. Ananse looked at the meat for a long while, and then it occurred to him that since the king was reputed to be the most eminent man in all the lands, and since only he ate of this strange meat, there must be a connection between the fame of the king and the meat of the python. Therefore, Ananse took a few pieces of the meat and ate them. He was careful to break off the meat in such a way as to avoid detection. He was surprised to find that the python meat tasted delicious! So each day, after clearing the table, Ananse would help himself to a few mouthfuls of python meat.

A couple of days after he started eating the python meat, Ananse realised that he had become more thoughtful than usual. When people spoke, the words acquired a clearer meaning for him than previously. What was even stranger was that he could understand the conversation of the animals and the whispers of the leaves. And there was no way of imagining how much animals held man in contempt!

One afternoon when he had completed his chores for the day and was resting in the shade of a tree, he overheard the dog, the cat and the goat discussing the folly of man. The dog wanted to understand why some people treated others like slaves when there was enough for all. The cat's concern had to do with why the enslaved allow such cruel exploitation to go on.

The goat laughed until his sides almost burst on the subject of man's arrogance; to think that man thought he was the wisest of all creatures when he could not even live in peace with his neighbours.

Ananse came to realise that he could also understand the language of the forest animals, and he thus asked them questions about the nature of their lives and the medicinal value of plants.

One day, after one of his trips to chat with the animals and huge trees of the forest, Ananse came home to find the whole palace in a state of agitation, with everyone shouting, pointing at him and calling him a thief. He was really confused, and before he had time to enquire what he was accused of having stolen, he was bound with strong ropes and brought before the king who was furious. Ananse's mind went immediately to the meat of the python and certain that someone had discovered his theft of the food, he made up his mind to confess.

However, the charge had nothing to do with meat, but everything to do with the disappearance of the queen's gold ring! Ananse was the major suspect because he was the only one who knew where the queen kept her jewellery. The queen had worn that particular ring when she attended a naming ceremony the previous day, and that was the last time she had seen the ring. Ananse was advised to confess to the crime or be killed. Ananse knew he had not stolen the ring and he was not prepared to suffer for a crime he had not committed. The more he protested his innocence, the more urgently the elders advised him to cut it all short by admitting his guilt, because the king was infallible. He had never been known to make mistakes in such matters.

While the accusations and denial continued, Ananse heard a chat between two ducks who had strayed by. One complained of the heavy feeling in his stomach which he attributed to swallowing that gold ring along with the leftovers after the feast of the naming ceremony. The other consoled her partner that maybe by the end of the day the ring would pass out of his digestive system.

As the executioners rushed to take Ananse away to be killed, Ananse asked for a last request which the angry king reluctantly granted. He accused the duck of stealing the ring of the king, a statement which really incensed the elders.

What does a duck want to do with a gold ring? Or was Ananse so overwhelmed with his sense of guilt that he was going crazy? However, Ananse insisted that the duck had the ring, and that it should be killed and its intestines examined. With a lot of impatience the duck was killed and can you imagine the look of surprise on the faces of the crowd when the gold ring was found safely lodged in its stomach!

The king realised that Ananse had been greatly wronged, and he asked what Ananse wanted as compensation. Instead of the riches that you may have asked for, Ananse asked that he become famous. He went on to prescribe how his fame was to be forever spread through stories told to both the young and the old.